To David McKee

First published in Great Britain by Andersen Press Ltd., 2005
Color separations by Fotoriproduzioni Grafiche, Verona
Printed and bound in Italy by Grafiche AZ, Verona
First American edition, 2006
1   3   5   7   9   10   8   6   4   2

www.fsgkidsbooks.com

Library of Congress Control Number: 2005928303

Pablo the Artist

SATOSHI KITAMURA

FARRAR STRAUS GIROUX NEW YORK

The members of Hoof Lane Art Club were excited.
There was to be an exhibition of their work and
everyone was busily painting—except for Pablo.
It was his dream to have a picture in an exhibition,
but now he stood in front of an empty canvas,
arms folded, looking troubled.

He had painted flowers in a vase,

a portrait of his friend,

and even an abstract painting.

Yet nothing looked right.
"I think I have artist's block!"
sighed Pablo.

"Why don't you go out and paint a landscape or something for a change?" suggested Miss Hippo during the tea break.

"Good idea!" agreed Leonardo the Lion. "In my view, a good landscape is the next best thing to a self-portrait."

Leonardo was very good at painting himself.

"Perhaps you're right," said Pablo. "I'll give it a try."

So the next morning Pablo woke up early and traveled out into the country.

After walking for some time
he found a lovely view:
a tall oak tree with a
stretch of green woods
in the background.

"This will make
a beautiful landscape,"
he said, and set up his easel
and canvas straightaway.

Pablo worked all morning. By noon he had painted the tree and some background.

"It looks all right, I think," said Pablo a little uncertainly. "At least it's a start. It'll get better after lunch."

Pablo had brought a big lunch box with him.

"An elephant cannot live by art alone," he sighed, and tucked hungrily into his sandwiches.

After the meal he felt drowsy.
So he decided to lie down
for a short while.
In no time at all,
he was fast asleep . . .

In the landscape a sheep was walking. He saw a canvas on an easel in the middle of the field.

"A painting?" he said. "How interesting!"

But even as he admired it, the sheep felt there was something wrong with the picture.

"I know," he said. "It's the grass! It looks completely tasteless!"

He picked up a paintbrush
and painted the grass
a delicious bright green.

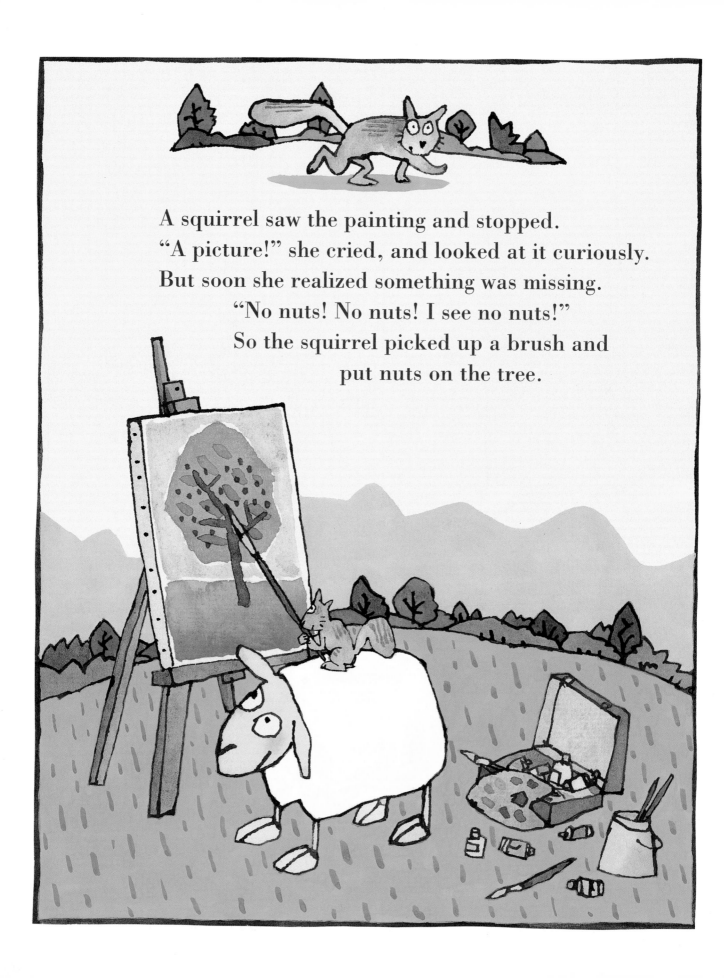

A squirrel saw the painting and stopped.
"A picture!" she cried, and looked at it curiously.
But soon she realized something was missing.
"No nuts! No nuts! I see no nuts!"
So the squirrel picked up a brush and
put nuts on the tree.

A bird flew down and peeked at the painting.
"If you want my opinion, it's hopeless," he said.
"No bird could spread its wings in such a bleak sky."
He took the brush in his beak and built up the sky
with a brilliant blue.

The next to arrive was a wild boar. She glanced at the canvas and stopped in her tracks.

"This won't do at all! Where is the shady green grove that I live in? How could the artist have missed it?"

And she added some darker green strokes to the horizon.

A swarm of bees came buzzing by.
"Buzz, buzz! Buzz, buzz! No flowers! No good!"
They lifted a brush and filled the field with flowers.

The painting looked much better now.
While the animals, the bird, and the bees
were admiring the result, a wolf strolled up.
He took a long, hard look at the canvas
but he didn't say a word.

"Hmmm . . ." the wolf said at last. "That's really cool, guys. But it can be even better, you know. Stand all together in front of the tree. And keep very still. This won't take too long."

Then he picked up a paintbrush and started to paint.

When the picture was finished, they gathered around to have a look. They were surprised by the way it had turned out, and applauded one after another.

"Gosh, this is wonderful!"

"Gorgeous!"

"I'm impressed."

"You're brilliant, Mr. Wolf!"

"Buzz buzz! Genius!"

Then they made their way home and disappeared . . .

Pablo woke up and yawned.

"What a strange dream," he said. "And what a beautiful painting . . . Now I know exactly what to do!"

He rushed back to his canvas and started to paint.

When at last it was done, Pablo packed up his things and made his way home.

When the exhibition opened, Pablo's painting was the star of the show and he was the toast of the town!

"It's wonderful!" "Gorgeous!" "I'm impressed!"
"You're brilliant, Pablo!"
"Genius!"

For Pablo it was a dream come true.